For Dr. Sherrie Hans, who wanted to
be a scientist when she was a girl,
and now is one —M.M.

To Rachael C., with gratitude,
and her son, Alex,
the Dinosaur Enthusiast —G.B.K.

Text copyright © 2018 by Margaret McNamara
Jacket art and interior illustrations copyright © 2018 by G. Brian Karas

Published in the United States by Schwartz & Wade Books,
an imprint of Random House Children's Books,
a division of Penguin Random House LLC, New York.

Schwartz & Wade Books and the colophon are trademarks of Penguin Random House LLC.

Visit us on the Web! rhcbooks.com

Educators and librarians, for a variety of teaching tools, visit us at RHTeachersLibrarians.com

Library of Congress Cataloging-in-Publication Data is available upon request.
ISBN 978-0-553-51143-7 (hc) — ISBN 978-0-553-51144-4 (lib. bdg.) — ISBN 978-0-553-51145-1 (ebook)

The text of this book is set in Century Schoolbook.
The illustrations were rendered in gouache, matte medium, and pencil on paper.
Book design by Rachael Cole

MANUFACTURED IN CHINA
2 4 6 8 10 9 7 5 3 1
First Edition

The author and artist wish to thank Taormina Lepore, paleontologist at
The Webb Schools and the Raymond M. Alf Museum of Paleontology; Liam Heins;
Lulu Mourning; and the curators of the American Museum of Natural History.

THE DINOSAUR EXPERT

by Margaret McNamara

illustrated by G. Brian Karas

schwartz & wade books · new york

Kimmy collected things so she could study them.
She collected rocks
and shells
and leaves and pebbles and feathers.
She even collected owl pellets. And she took them apart.
But of all the things Kimmy collected, fossils were her favorite.

That's why Kimmy was happy that Mr. Tiffin's class was at the natural history museum for a dinosaur field trip.

She had been there many times. She knew so much about dinosaurs. She couldn't wait to share.

"Whoa!" said Alex as soon as they walked into the first room.
"Dinosaur fight!"

Kimmy stepped forward. "The big one is a *Barosaurus*," she said.
"She's a plant eater. And the small, fierce one is an *Allosaurus*.

"The *Allosaurus* can move fast. But the *Barosaurus* has a super-powerful tail," continued Kimmy. "She'd use it to protect her baby."

"You know a lot about dinosaurs," said Jake.

"I love fossils," Kimmy said. "I want to be a scientist when I grow up."

"Girls aren't scientists," Jake said.

And Kimmy stopped talking.

In the next room, there were big photographs of old-fashioned people. Some of them were out in the desert. Some of them were standing with dinosaur bones.

"Does anyone know what a dinosaur scientist is called?" asked Mr. Tiffin.

Kimmy knew.

"A paleontologist," said Elinor.

"Right," said Mr. Tiffin. "Paleontologists study fossils. These pictures show paleontologists from long ago. Dinosaur scientists are still looking for dinosaur fossils nowadays, all over the world."

Kimmy studied the photographs. She read the fossil hunters' names out loud.

"Edward Drinker Cope. Earl Douglass. O. C. Marsh."

"See?" said Jake.

The next room was Kimmy's favorite. Every case had a different set of dinosaur bones. She knew which ones were from the Triassic period, when dinosaurs first walked the earth. And which were from the Jurassic period, the age of the giant dinosaurs. And which were from the Cretaceous period, when dinosaurs shared the planet with so many new species of mammals and insects and birds and flowering plants.

Mr. Tiffin led the class to a plaster cast of a tiny dinosaur skeleton.

Kimmy knew what it was right away. *"Archaeopteryx,"* she whispered. "Jurassic."

"This is an *Archaeopteryx,* from the Jurassic period," Mr. Tiffin said. "Look at that skeleton. Does it remind you of anything?"

Kimmy wanted to tell the class
that this dinosaur was a relative of
a bird. She wanted to say that birds
and dinosaurs are related, and that
some dinosaurs even had feathers.

She put her hand up.
"Looks like a dancing rabbit!"
Molly shouted.
"With a monkey tail!" called Jake.
Everybody laughed.

Kimmy put her hand down.

While Tara drew jawbones and Elinor recited a dinosaur poem, Kimmy studied an *Oviraptor*'s nest. After a while, Mr. Tiffin came over. They looked at the exhibit quietly together.

"Scientists used to think these dinos stole eggs," said Kimmy. "But then they realized that *Oviraptors* sat on their eggs, to protect them."

"I'm sure the class would like to hear that," said Mr. Tiffin.

"Maybe some other time," said Kimmy.

Jake ran ahead to the next room. "Check this out!" he called.
It was a special exhibit.

"This is the biggest dinosaur ever!" said Robert. "A titanosaur!"
"It doesn't even fit in the room!" said Alex.

"Kimmy," said Mr. Tiffin, "you might want to see this."

Kimmy went over and took a look.
There was a dinosaur she had never
seen before, called *Gasparinisaura*.
She read all about it.

GASPARINISAURA CINCOSALTENSIS

Found recently, this herbivore was
graceful and very fast. Scientists
believe Gasparinisaura cincosaltensis
lived in groups, as adults, youths, and
babies were found within a small area.
It dates from approximately ninety
million years ago. It was named in honor
of Zulma Brandoni de Gasparini.

And then she saw the
photos of Dr. Brandoni de
Gasparini.

Kimmy smiled wide.

"I thought you'd like her,"
said Mr. Tiffin.

One picture showed
Dr. Brandoni de Gasparini
hunting for fossils.

"Fossil hunting is a dusty
business," said Mr. Tiffin.

"I love dust!" said Kimmy.

There was another
photo, of Dr. Brandoni de
Gasparini with test tubes.
And one of the doctor
winning an award.

"Awesome," said Jake.

"*Really* awesome," said
Kimmy. "She is so cool!"

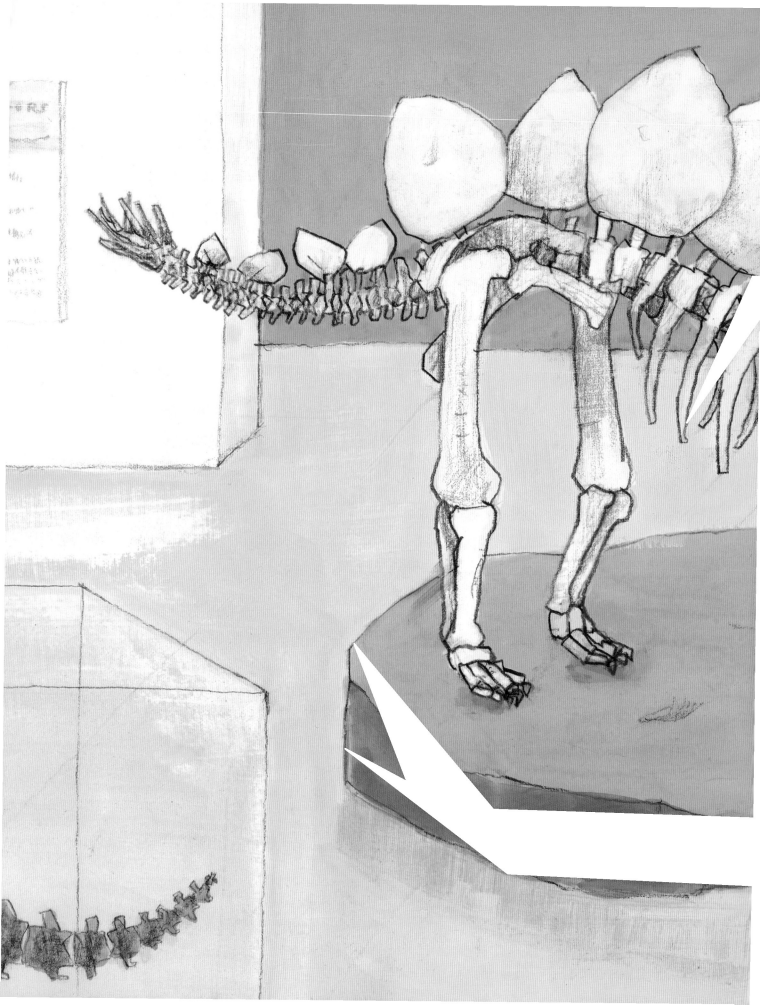

In the next three rooms, Kimmy kept talking. She told the class a lot. "This guy's brain was tiny! People used to think it must have had another brain hiding somewhere, to control such a big body," she said. "But it only had one."

"These look like raptor toes," said Kimmy. "Some raptors needed three toes and others only used two."

"Interesting," said Molly.

"Finger bones are interesting, too," Kimmy said. "Earlier raptors had five fingers and later raptors had three."

"How come?" asked Jake.

"They evolved," Kimmy said. "They kept what they needed and changed what they didn't."

"We're always evolving," said Mr. Tiffin.

"That's a dinosaur mummy," said Kimmy. "It was preserved for sixty-five million years before anybody found it. You can even see its skin."

"You make these dinos sound so real," said Jeremy.

"It's almost like they're alive," said Anna.

"Imagine what *that* field trip would be like!" said Mr. Tiffin.

"Okay, class, back to reality," said Mr. Tiffin. "Time to head home."

As the class took a last look at the dinosaurs, Kimmy turned to Mr. Tiffin. "That titanosaur was amazing," she said. "But I liked the one named for Dr. Brandoni de Gasparini best."

"Me too," said Mr. Tiffin.

"When I grow up, I want to be just like her,"
Kimmy said.

"I think," said Mr. Tiffin, "you already are."

MY FAVORITE PALEONTOLOGISTS
by Kimmy

It turns out there are loads of women paleontologists. Even some girls!
Here's one from the olden days....

Mary Anning was one of the first fossil scientists ever! She lived from 1799 to 1847, on the coast of England. She found thousands of fossils from the Jurassic period, including the first full *Plesiosaurus* skeleton. She was also the first person to identify an ichthyosaur. There's a famous rhyme about her: "She sells seashells by the seashore. . . ." Mary Anning, however, should be remembered as a scientist, not as a tongue-twister. ☺

But all these scientists are working now!

Karen Chin is an American paleontologist who loved studying living organisms when she was young. Then she got interested in dinosaur coprolites. A coprolite is fossilized poop! Poop gives us all kinds of information about what dinosaurs ate and the ecosystem in which they lived. Poop rocks!

Anusuya Chinsamy-Turan won the South African Woman of the Year Award for her work studying dinosaurs and other extinct animals. She is proud to have been on teams that have named five different dinosaurs, including *Nqwebasaurus thwazi,* the first dinosaur that uses the Xhosa language in its name. (Xhosa is a language spoken in southern Africa by the Bantu people—you learn a lot when you start reading about paleontology!)

Daisy Morris started looking for fossils when she was just three years old. Then, when she was four, she found an important fossil on the beach near her home on the Isle of Wight, in England. It was part of a new species of pterosaur! Four years after her discovery, the new dino was named in Daisy's honor. Its official name is *Vectidraco daisymorrisae*. That is so cool.

Stephanie Pierce is a vertebrate paleontologist who grew up in Alberta, Canada, where she hunted for fossils on the badlands. She says that when she's on a dig and she wants to know if something is really a fossil . . . she licks it! That clears away the dirt and reveals the bone's inner pores. Fun!

Mr. Tiffin told me to add there is NO LICKING ALLOWED (until you are a grown-up paleontologist).

Lisa White is a micropaleontologist. That means she studies fossils at a microscopic level. She was not so interested in dinosaurs when she was little—she was a photographer before she was a paleontologist. Now she takes fossil pictures with her electron microscope.

And best of all . . .

Zulma Brandoni de Gasparini is a paleontologist from Argentina. She is one of the very few Latina women who studied science in her country in the 1960s and 1970s. She discovered the *Gasparinisaura* and was also part of the team that found a giant reptile called *Dakosaurus andiniensis* that lived over 135 million years ago. It resembles the modern-day crocodile, except it had fins and lived entirely underwater. She tells her grandchildren about her adventures hunting dinos!

Mary Anning photo reproduced by permission of the Geological Society of London; Karen Chin photo courtesy of Carey A. Cass/University of Colorado; Anusuya Chinsamy-Turan photo courtesy of Peter Rudden; Daisy Morris photo courtesy of Daisy Morris; Stephanie Pierce photo courtesy of MCZ/Harvard University; Lisa White photo courtesy of Laura B. Childs/University of California, Berkeley; Zulma Brandoni de Gasparini photo courtesy of National University of La Plata.